-Des

By Benji

Cover design by:

Hroðgar Yaxley

Contents.

Introduction from the Author.

I remember some years back being asked
"what's your opinion, Ben?", and at the time
knowing full well that the answer given would
either be met by nods of approval, or wagging
fingers and hostility. Needless to say, it was the
latter that I was confronted with, and I was
pleased when I could finally give leave and go
home.
You are probably wondering what the question
entailed? Well, like so many froth inducing
responses, it was caused by a mixture of
political, social, and cultural topics, each one
snowballing into monstrous debates that spiral
out of control whenever you meet the politically
self-righteous!
It's odd isn't it, that more often than not when
people know that they're not going to like the
answer to their questions, they feel more
inclined to want to ask you, almost as if they
want to be offended! It's this realisation that has
caused me to slowly remove myself from the
limited, and somewhat pathetic political sphere
of conversations, and move into a more
meditative and observant position that allows
me to watch and learn, rather than rant and rave.

This 'want' to be offended reminds me of the kinds of people who pay a lady in latex underwear to beat them with a riding crop, and afterwards, despite feeling satisfied, they come away with cuts and bruises and in worse shape than when they started! This need to be offended carries the same attitude, and has all the hallmarks of self-induced persecution. There isn't really an aggressor, but for some reason they want one! Is this somehow to make them feel as if they share something in common with the truly oppressed? You could speculate on this till the cows come home…

Why have I felt the need to tell you this? Well, from left to right it's the same, and in answer to the question above, I disagree with the political institutions as they stand today. They offer nothing except the promise of further deception, corruption, and confusion, and when these things are brought together, they can create a very powerful, very corrosive environment. The infrastructure of the western world and its *logos* has slowly, and increasingly, made a mockery out of what it means to be a human being.

Just take a look at the sort of people who get the air time on tv, or the supposed 'influencers' online, for the most part they are twisted versions of the human form, and seem alien when you take them out of context. Do you really think that the universal blueprint, created at the beginning of time, really factored this in as a part of its design? To offer an opposing argument, perhaps we need corruption to help give birth to new meanings and new ways of thinking. You could even say that the more advanced the animal, the more overwhelming their destruction needs to be, and a highly 'self-aware' being needs a highly 'self-aware' destruction.

Either way, would you feel happy subjecting your children to all this? Would you be happy to see them get tangled up in a web of self-abuse, sexual addiction, pollution (both mental and physical) and anxiety inducing work environments? Because look at our world now, look at what has been created.

There is a gaudy, plastic coated world out there, and I mean that in both a physical and mental sense.

Everything is shoddy and poorly managed. Everything is reduced to monetary worth, not spiritual value. In this world, even the ultra-rich are bankrupt, and you can have all the money in the world, but if you don't have a healthy dose of morality, wrapped up in ethical fortitude, you're very poor indeed.

Look at me! Even I'm becoming sanctimonious…

Can you see how divisive a question can be? Can you see how just an opinion can open up a whole can of worms? Far be it from me to tell you what is right and what is wrong, but the story that you are about to read is in many ways an answer to the above question, "What's your opinion, Ben?"

In an attempt to present a philosophical view of the world we inhabit today, I found myself writing not from a contemporary stance, but from a future perspective. It seemed to me to be the natural and most logical place to start, in order for me to 'reflect.'

If I was to try and explain what point I am trying to get across, I feel I would probably fall short of the mark, not because I don't understand the nature of what I have written, but because I have invested so much of myself in what you are about to read. I feel I would be coming at it from the ultimately subjective, rather than the objective, which would be necessary in explaining my motivations. This is also the reason for me writing in a fictitious, narrative form. I didn't (and I hope I haven't) want to come across as preachy. So many philosophical ideas/books do this! By framing philosophy as an instruction manual, much like that of Marx or Hegel, you end up getting the feeling you're being told what you should and shouldn't do. I wanted to avoid this, and leave the question of what I am trying to say 'open'. I hope, by framing my ideas in fiction, that I have been able to do this.

Don't get me wrong, I would never want to downplay the great achievements of philosophers before me, or seek to make what I say seem like the be all and end all of the matter, but what I have sought to do is bring you a 'perspective' and a way of viewing what could be the possible consequences of our actions today, by looking not only at a possible future, but also a past that relates to that future. A past that is ultimately our future, if you catch my drift? The inspiration for this book came from a deep desire to be able to contextualize what I think and feel, and to place those thoughts in a fictional reality, to see how they would play out.

Once again, I have been met with questions such as 'What do you think?' and I have always answered them, rather erroneously, with what I 'don't' think. This is often the case. We are only too happy to tell people what we disagree with in great detail, but when it comes to what we actually think, we are often a little vague, and find ourselves talking about other people's ideas, rather than our own. Here, I hope I'm able to present to you 'My' thoughts.

In all honesty, I'm uninterested in other people's politics and dogmas, and in a world where everyone has an opinion, you find yourself struggling to make sense of all the words and wishy-washy statements. And yet despite this, many of my views and opinions are built from the bricks laid down by those before me, and I find myself looking to the 'greats' for a sense of understanding.

This here is an attempt to get to the point and understand! Well, at least part of the way. That isn't to say that this is a completely unique work of philosophy or fiction, as it is quite obvious that there are similarities between Thomas More's *Utopia,* and Plato's *Critias,* etc… But as you will see, I have tried to lend a modern perspective on these ideas, and flesh out some of the finer details as I see them.

Of course, with a work such as this, I could go on *Ad infinitum*, trying to explain all the little details, and all the different avenues that this future could go down, but the issue here would be that if everything was explained it would leave nothing to the readers imagination, or serve as an idea for others to 'play' with. So, as you will see, the gaps in the narrative are there for a reason. In fact, the gaps are there for you, a place for you to insert your own perspectives, and your own thoughts, rather than me telling you what to think and what to believe. I can't stand that kind of attitude, and it's something I think we've all experienced ourselves at some point in our own lives.

With all the pretention of philosophy aside, I hope you enjoy reading this as much as I did writing it, and that at the end of the day you can see that it's just a story, but a story with a very deep human *geist*. As such, it is to be handled with care and consideration, and not used, like so many works of its type, as a half-baked blueprint for the way we 'should' be, but rather as a picture for what 'could' be.

B. Elliott.

This book is dedicated to my Mother and Father, who in their own separate ways, inspired me to speak with my own voice.

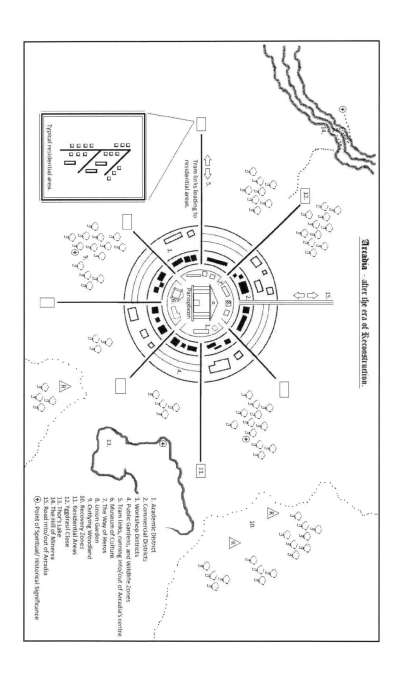

Arcadia - after the era of Reconstruction.

Typical residential area.

Tram links leading to residential areas.

Panopticon

1. Academic District
2. Commercial Districts
3. Workshop Districts
4. Public Gardens, and Wildlife Zones
5. Tram links, running into/out of Arcadia's centre
6. Museum of Culture
7. The Way of Heros
8. Union Garden
9. Outlying Woodland
10. Recovery Zones
11. Residential Areas
12. Yggdrasil Close
13. Thor's Lake
14. The Hill of Minerva
15. Road into/out of Arcadia
⊕ Point of Spiritual/ Historical Significance

are begotten, they

The Polybius Effect

*"When an individual evaluates events around them based
on their social-political or ideological beliefs, rather than on
the facts at their disposal."*

*The Polybius Effect is normally attributed to those who act
as a result of indoctrination, or lack the necessary critical
faculties to assess the situation for what it really is.*

(Fragment of text from the codex 'Noble Title' by Obi Tellnett.)
cat no: 1112.06

nd he answered is nations call, and took up the position appointed to him by the Senat
obody douted his skill and capability for the task at hand, and in the following months
he made good his appointment, and defended Rome from it's invaders.
When he had completed his charge, he willingly handed the power back to the Senate,
for he understood that the greatness of the nation and its institutions were more importan
than the prestige of a single man.

or his love, he unders

(Fragment of text. An account of the life of an unknown Roman Citizen)
cat no: 2627.03

Think always of the universe as one living creature,
comprising one substance and one soul: how all is absorbed
into this one consciousness; how a single implulse governs all
its actions; how all things collaborate in all that happ

carryi

(Fragment of text. Of unknown origin)
cat no: 4041.31

Set in Stone.

"Settle on the kind of person you want to be, and stick to it…"
(**Epictetus** – Enchiridion)

Tom was just finishing up at his school's Union Garden, one of many gardens placed in or on the outskirts of secondary schools and colleges as a form of extra-curricular activity. It had been a bit of a hard day as far as Tom was concerned. Maths in the morning, followed by English, Philosophy, and Environmental Studies in the afternoon, but despite this, he had gotten a lot out of the day, and had really enjoyed Mr Stevens arguments about the new Tram-Link Initiatives of the last hundred years. History had always interested Tom, and whilst he finished cleaning his fork and hedge clippers, he contemplated on what the *Pretanic Isles* had been like before the Tipping Wars. As he did so, a whistle blew, signalling the end of that days gardening session. Tom took his tools over to the Union Garden tool shed and joined the hustle and bustle of other students trying to get their garden implements onto the right racks and shelves. Once the shed had been locked up by one of the senior students, they all said their goodbyes, and dispersed in their various directions home. Only Tom hung around for a bit, breathing in a deep lung full of clear, sweet summer air, whilst looking down on the afternoon's accomplishments.

Leeks, Cabbages, Tomatoes, and a series of pyramid shaped structures built from canes that held up the tangle of green beans growing around them, their colours enhanced by the afternoon sun, making them appear more like emeralds than beans. Despite the time, the sun was still high, and sent a satisfyingly warm blanket down on his shoulders. He looked around, and took in his surroundings. What an accomplishment it must have been, he thought to himself, looking up at the school. Built in the Neo-Classical style, the school looked more like something you might have seen in a book on the ancient Greeks, with its wide and imposing pediment, and the elegant symmetrically placed Ionic columns. Like all the major institutes of learning, they were all purpose built in the centre of towns and cities during the era of Reconstruction, and served as a focal point for all citizens, almost like a source of inspiration, at least that's what Tom always thought, and he had to admit that going to school felt like a real honour, rather than an imposition, but then, that's what everyone thought.

Ω

He picked up his bag, and made his way out of the Union Garden, and over a small bridge which linked it with the grounds of the school proper. He passed the school and some of the administrative buildings on the grounds, all built in the Trabeated style, and walked down the main entrance path paved in cobble stone, locally referred to as the 'Way of Heroes', which was flanked either side by statues of famous citizens who had contributed to the era of Reconstruction, and the noble philosophers who had ended the Tipping Wars. Tom stopped for a moment, and looked up at one of these figures. It was his is favourite, Dr G.F. Perkins. The small plaque beneath stated *'Dr G.F. Perkins, Mathematician, and Philosopher. The man whose great vision ended the dark age of humanity.'* The statue was made from a shiny black fibre composite, tall and striking. In one hand, Dr Perkins held a huge open book, whilst the other hand pointed off in the direction of the school. The look on his face was hard to make out, but it had the look of strictness crossed with quiet contemplation, and to Tom's mind, had the air of the paternal. His beard was long, and he was adorned in the robes often worn during the classical era. Tom's eyes met those of the striking figure standing before him, and a tear ran down the cheek of the young boy, but not tears of sadness, tears of joy and reverent respect. You might wonder at this response from a boy of seventeen, but this was an often-seen reaction from the youth of these times, and songs were often sung during the festival seasons, when harvests were brought in, or when the ancestors were being honoured in the great celebrations of Anthesterion, which evoked these emotions, in the young and old alike.

Tom was aware that there had been great turmoil in the past, but his teachers had only alluded to it very briefly in history lessons. He knew though, that when he came of age he would be made privy to the 'The Great Knowledge', something that was kept from children in the interests of preserving an attribute of great importance, something only the young possess. Innocence.

Ω

When Tom finally reached the end of the cobbled route, he had reached the end of the academic district of town, and was now in the commercial district. This was another feature of modern life, which had come to be accepted as the norm in Pretania. In most of the major towns and cities everything had been restructured with the academic institutions at the centre, and Arcadia was no exception.

Circling the academic district was the commercial district, which again was designed in the classical style, and comprised of shops, and administrative buildings. Nothing in the commercial district that was sold came from abroad, and pretty much most of the items for sale were of practical and utilitarian use. Even the shelves of toy stores were stocked with items made locally in one or other of Arcadia's craft-based workshops.

Surrounding the commercial district was the workshop and trade-based industries, normally comprising of small family run businesses, and cooperatives specializing in anything from hand forged iron gates, to furniture and building supplies, all made in house with locally sourced materials. This created the effect of making each town in Pretania responsible for the essential items it needed, whilst at the same time maintaining a sense of awareness for the raw materials consumed. If something then could be reused, it would be. Many a time, outside people's homes, you would see the remnants of some piece of furniture that had seen its day being used for something else, such as framing for raised beds in the front garden, or table legs being used to grow plants up.

Ω

The last two surrounding areas were made up of residential streets, rural space and the 'Recovery Zones' beyond. If seen from above, the entire town would have looked like a series of circles, one inside of another.

All of the districts of Arcadia were linked by a well-planned, and highly efficient tram link service that ran on solar energy, generated by solar panels on top of the commercial buildings, and fed directly into a distributer that in turn transported it to the overhead lines linked to the trams. It was one of these particular trams that Tom was now waiting for at the tram stop.

The tram he was waiting for was a number four, so he sat at the stop patiently, and read a book on Charles Dickens that he had been given as home work. 'Excuse me young man, do you know when the number four is due?' Tom looked up, and noticed a small, hunched old lady, with an even smaller, and even more hunched old man holding her arm.

Tom smiled and said, 'It should be here any minute, it's the one I'm catching too'. The elderly lady nodded politely, as did her partner, and they both sat beside Tom on the bench. A few moments passed, and Tom could feel the old lady looking in his direction. 'Is that Dickens you're reading there?' she asked. 'Yes' replied Tom, 'in fact it's my home work.' The little old lady smiled, and nodded again. 'It's so lovely to see that young people haven't forgotten their forbears, and the people who've made this country great. You know, if it hadn't been for people like Dickens, Hilton, Orwell, or even Plato, I don't know what sort of mess we would be in today. It's young boys and girls like you who are the future. As for my husband and I, we've served are time, and done our duty, and for that the *Fellowship* takes care of us.'

The Fellowship was an organization that cared for elderly citizens who had no family to look after them. It was made up of a body of volunteers, under the guidance of a *Censor* from the Panopticon, who made regular house calls to clean, cook, and serve as a source of company. The Fellowship even helped individuals who wished to end their lives. This was only ever performed under special circumstances, and you needed to be over the age of 65, and show good cause that you were no longer of any use to society, and that no one was relying on you either financially, or emotionally. It would then be down to the Panopticon, and a selection of 5 members of your neighborhood, to vote on what action should be taken.

Ω

Tom felt a little embarrassed at being referred to as 'the future', and wasn't entirely sure how to respond to such a remark. Luckily, he didn't have to, as the brass bell of the tram coming up the road signalled its arrival. Tom put his book back in his bag, and asked the old lady and her husband if they would like a hand getting into the carriage.

Ω

As the number four slowly made its way through the various districts, Tom sat at the back of the carriage and watched the sunny world outside pass by. It was interesting to think that it had only been thirty years since the last car was seen on the roads, and even longer still since the rock fuel vehicles were even used. Most of them now were either in museums, or had been recycled into something more useful.

Only citizens who had permission from the Panopticon could use vehicles, and even then, they were fueled by electricity generated by small windmills attached to the houses where the vehicle was registered, fed via a cable directly into the car or van. Internally, they had little in the way of comforts, and were purely made in the interests of utility, not prestige. To get one you had to work in a rural area of the country doing state sanctioned farming or forestry work. If not, the reasons for needing one would have to be exceptional, and your petition would have to go to a board of specialists at the Panopticon. It wasn't just the pollution and congestion of vehicles that was on people's minds, but noise as well. Noise had been linked to so many forms of physical and mental health problems, that it was considered to be in the interests of all citizens to keep traffic to an absolute minimum.

That being said, the carriage of the tram was full of conversation and laughter.

Ω

A man and woman sitting in front of Tom were talking about the upcoming Festival of Lights with great excitement, and a middle aged lady opposite him was engrossed in conversation with a young girl in front of her about child birth techniques, explaining that a water birth is always far better, as it makes the transition into this world far easier for the baby. Everyone was in good spirits, including the little old lady and her husband, who sat at the front of the carriage, periodically smiling at each other, whilst quietly and gently holding hands.

Ω

When Tom finally reached his stop half an hour later, he hoped off, thanked the driver, and walked the last few minutes or so to his home. The Street Tom lived on was called Yggdrasil Close, and a large Elm tree was positioned at its centre. Each house on the close was built in a similar fashion, and bore the traditional steep roofs, and exposed wooden supports you might find a house in a fairy tale having, all of which were sustainably built from local materials. Tom walked slowly past each house, looking at the flowers and crops in his fellow neighbours' gardens. How beautiful and ripe everything looked, he thought, bending down for a moment and smelling a rose.

As he did, a voice called out from behind him. 'Hey Tom! Am I still coming over for dinner tonight?' Tom spun round and looked up at the top window of the house across the road. It was George, Tom's best friend. Tom chuckled, 'I'm surprised you're not already sitting at the table!' George disappeared from the window, and moments later came bounding out of the house towards Tom, his shirt half hanging out of his trousers, and his hair all frantic and knotted like a bird's nest. 'What's your Mother cooking tonight!?' asked George, with great enthusiasm. 'I think it's some sort of bake' replied Tom, 'at least, I hope so'. George flung his arm round Tom's shoulders, and they walked and talked the last few yards back to Tom's.

He often wondered if George ever washed. It wasn't that he smelt bad, but he almost always had dirt under his nails, and the knees of his trousers were nearly always muddy or scuffed with grass stains. It made sense, because unlike Tom's Mother and Father who worked at the Science Academy, Georges Mother and Father worked on the Permaculture Reserve a few miles away, and George, obviously picking up his parents love of wildlife, spent most of his spare time down by the river on his hands and knees, watching the newts and frogs.

Periodically he would come home soaking wet, with scratches and bruises, where he'd fallen in. It was these strange qualities that endeared Tom to George, and he loved him like a brother.

Ω

The two boys finally reached the front door of Tom's house. Tom turned the latch, and the pair went indoors, laughing as they did so, shutting the quaint ledge and brace door behind them.

If I Could Marry Her.

"Kindness and Love, the most curative herbs and agents in human intercourse"
*(**Nietzsche** – Aphorisms on Love and Hate.)*

Tom's home was a simple affair, and was laid out in much the same way as a country cottage, with low beams, exposed floorboards, a comfortable living room, and a small tight staircase that took you up into the cosy bedrooms above. The real soul of the house though was the kitchen, with its pressed fibre tile floor, designed to look like terracotta, the large range with pots and pans hanging around it, and the dark oak dining table at its centre, which always rocked up and down if you put too much pressure on one corner, sometimes causing cups and jugs of water to be sent flying into the laps of whoever might be unlucky enough to be in their path.

Ω

The two boys set the table, while Frey, Tom's Mother, brought the sweet-smelling bake out of the oven. Frey was a tall woman, with golden blonde hair, and the deepest of blue eyes. She wore her hair up in plats, and her face was beautiful and strong.

She was, in many regards, the ideal woman, and beneath her motherly exterior beat the heart of an intellectual, who could hold her own in any conversation, debate, or argument. Her abilities didn't end there either, and she could often be seen in the garden, sowing seeds, chopping wood, and when at work, organising everyone in her calm, but authoritative manner.

Ω

Tom's Father, who had evidently smelt the food from upstairs, had come down, and entered the kitchen to inspect the progress. Paul was the same height as Frey, and had a sturdy chiselled face, brown hair, brown eyes, and light weight rimless glasses. He was a jolly chap though, and there was nothing he didn't know about anything! It was because of his great diversity of knowledge, and his supreme intellect, that he was being considered for a position at the Panopticon, as a specialist.

Specialists were part of the governing body within the Panopticon, and were drawn from a wide cross section of society. In effect they made the laws, and those laws were in turn handed down to magistrates, who would put the laws into action.

'Come on then everyone' Frey called, 'dinners up'. They all sat down, and after they had linked hands around the table, bowed their heads, and paid homage to the Gods and ancestors, as was the custom, they began to eat. George set about shovelling down the roaring hot food, whilst Paul and Frey looked at him with complete amusement, but not surprise. This was George all over, and he was always like this when you put food in front of him.

Ω

Tom ate in his usual completive manner, taking time to chew his food, and only spoke at the table if either of his parents addressed him. 'So Tom, how was school today. Did you get your results for the Summer exams?' Paul asked, in a nonchalant fashion. 'Not yet, no. Dr Hendriksen said we would probably have to wait until after the Festival of Lights' Tom replied, with a certain amount of relief in his voice.
'I think his wife is making garlands for their local celebrations, and he's helping her with something to do with that,' Continued Tom.

Frey turned to Paul, remembering her duties to the local community, 'Thank you for reminding me Tom, the communal Elm outside will need to be dressed at some point, and I must ask Georges Mother if she'll be available to help me make up some decorations.' Frey turned to George, who was still in the throngs of eating, 'Could you ask your mother for me when you get home this evening?' George looked up, his mouth full of food, 'ser thin Fre, ul let er no'. The three of them all looked at each other, hoping that someone would have understood what the scruffy boy had just said, then spontaneously all burst out laughing, and George, who had forgotten himself, lent his elbow on the corner of the table, and sent a glass of water into his lap, which as far as everyone else was concerned, just added to the hilarity.

Ω

An hour passed, and by the time dinner was finished, and conversations had reached their natural conclusion, all at the table started clearing up. George helped Frey with the washing up, and brought in a pale of water from the communal well at the end of the close, as none of the residential houses had plumed water.

Again, this was as per Panopticon decree, and after the era of reconstruction residential areas had all been built with communal facilities at their core, such as communal wells and water pumps. This wasn't just in the interests of communal living and bringing people together, but also served as a way of making sure people didn't abuse the natural resources they had. The Panopticon had named it the *Apstemius Consilium*, reminding people of the importance of moderation in all things.

Ω

Tom helped his Father put all the dishes away, and clean down the dining table. Any left overs Tom took out into the back garden, and put on top of the composter. When all the work was completed, the four sat out on the back porch with cups of mint tea, and looked out over the garden. Tom and George sat on the step that led into the garden, while Frey and Paul sat in small wicker armchairs next to each other, holding hands. It was a beautiful evening, and the sun was stretching out the last of its deep red rays, before it would eventually disappear behind the hills in the distance.

The garden was still full of the fresh sounds and smells of the day. The aroma of jasmine and herbs permeated the air, and the low croaking of frogs could be heard coming up from the stream at the far end of the garden.

A profound, dark, wild blanket of warmth still hung in the air, like the spirit of some forgotten past, waiting to be made whole again, and its loving arms laid around the shoulders of the small group, keeping them safe, as if it were the spirit of Mother Nature herself. You could almost feel the garden breathing.

Even in the darkness, everything was full of life. When Paul and Frey had finally gone inside and made their way to bed, the two boys sat alone and talked. As you would expect, their conversation focused on school, friends, and girls. '…what about Sarah?' asked George. 'What about her?' Tom replied, knowing full well what he was asking about. 'Would you marry Sarah?' George asked again, this time with a little more force. Tom pretended to think for a moment, as if the idea had never crossed his mind.

'Well, let's face it, she's probable the most beautiful in our school, and when it comes to her knowledge of wildlife, I don't think anyone has her beat, well at least not in our year.' They sat in silence for a moment, both evidently contemplating their fellow class mate, until George finally piped up.

'If I could marry her, we would have lots of children, and I would keep Guinea pigs in the back garden, while she made seed balls for the birds, and…well, that's it'.

George had the amazing ability to start sentences that would seem to be going somewhere, but would more than often end abruptly, often to Tom's amusement.

'Would you now?' Tom replied, 'Some plan!'. George looked at him incredulously, 'Ok then, what would you do if you married her?'. Tom looked off down the end of the garden, into the blackness, and took a long draw of air through his nostrils. 'Well for starters, lots of children would be out of the question. Seeing as I'm probably going to be an academic one of these days, I'll legally only be allowed one child, and on top of that it looks as though she'll be following in her parents footsteps and working in the Recovery Zone, so I don't think it would really work out…'

Ω

An hour or so had passed, and George waved goodbye as he walked up the close, and across the road to is house. Tom stood on the front door step for a few minutes and thought about what George had said. 'Lots of children and Guinea pigs'. The idea seemed ridiculous, but at the back of Toms mind there was a niggling jealousy.

Academic couples would only ever be allowed to have one child, where-as couples who worked the woodland areas, took care of animals or were involved in manual trades could have as many as they wished, so long as they could provide for them. Tom understood the reasons why, academic couples tend to have academic children, and outdoorsy types tended to have outdoorsy children. Tom recalled what his father had once said. "You only need a few people to come up with the ideas, but you need lots of pairs of hands to make it work."

Tom finally shut the front door, and made his way up the small wooden staircase to his bedroom. He climbed into bed, and had only been lying there for a few minutes when his eyelids slowly began to close, and he drifted into a deep, dreamless sleep.

Like Thunder.

"I will plant my feet on that step where my parents put me as a child"
(St. Augustine – _Confessions_)

August had finally arrived and the summer holidays were in full swing. Tom, George, and George's four sisters had all spent the day out in the Designated Woodland, which had been selected by the Panopticon for its outstanding beauty, as well as its clean, and unadulterated soil. Some areas which fell into the remit of the Recovery Zones were obviously off limits, but certain areas that had been made available were thought of as very important for the health and wellbeing of its local residents who, if they properly treated them, had uninterrupted access. Children especially were encouraged to get as much fresh air as possible, and keep themselves fit and active. Georges Father and Mother had often remarked, 'Lazy Mind, Lazy Body, Lazy Child', often followed up by saying that society can't afford to carry dead weight. 'Everyone, no matter what their capacity must do their bit, however small!'

Ω

The assembled gang were busying themselves with a few rounds of Thunder, a game that involved one person playing the role of thunder, whilst the others hid behind trees with their eyes closed. When 'thunder' had found someone, they would have to try their hardest not to scream or flinch when thunder clapped their hands in front of their face. George loved playing thunder, and delighted in making his sisters jump.

Sowulo, despite being the youngest, never did. She often said that it was because she thought of herself as lightning, "and why would lightning be afraid of thunder?" Tom on the other hand enjoyed the tip toeing through the woods, trying his hardest not to tread on a twig, and thus alerting others to his presence. To Tom it felt as if he was a hunter, stalking through the woods like the people of old. A man alone against the elements.

$$\Omega$$

By the end of the day, when everyone was walking back home over the meadow, with the sun drifting down towards the horizon, they all chatted about the following day's events. Sowulo, and her older sisters Jenny, Sissy, and Heather held hands and skipped merrily along, talking as they did so about what lanterns they would carry tomorrow morning, while Tom and George talked about the ceremonial daggers their fathers carried, and what had to be done when they reached the great megalith at the top of the hill. It was the same conversation that was had every year in the lead up to the festival of lights, and the same conversations were being had in a variety of different places, by different people, across the country.

Ω

As the group dispersed, George went home with his sisters, and Tom continued along the close, waving goodbye as he went.
The entirety of Yggdrasil close was a buzz of activity. People were hanging bunting made from leaves outside their homes, while others were bringing out large carved statues of woodland creatures and mythical beasts and dotting them around the pavement.

Some of Tom's neighbours were bringing out large barrels, along with big wooden tables and benches, while an old man was carrying a box filled with wind instruments, and another, who was following behind carried a big bundle of decorations, evidently destined to be hung on the Elm tree along with his Mothers decorations. Everyone was doing something. Tom offered to help carry a few boxes for June Summers, an old lady who lived at number four, and she gratefully accepted his offer. 'You are a dear, Tom. I bring these decorations out every year, and every year they get just that little bit heavier. It's the joy that it brings though that makes it all worthwhile'. Tom put the boxes down by the tree, and asked if she wanted a hand putting them out, but June's pride had already been marked. 'No thank you Tom, I think I can manage it from here'.

June's husband had died a few years previous, and as you can imagine, the pair of them always put the decorations out together. She was a small lady, but there was a tenacity in her eyes, and a determinedness in her chin that Tom was not prepared to question. 'I'll see you tomorrow' said Tom, as he made his way across the road, and up the path towards his house.

As Tom came in through the front door, his father was in the hall busying himself with his dark brown robes, taking a stiff brush to them and getting rid of a years-worth of dust. 'Ah Tom by boy, out in the woods again? Better get your stuff ready for tomorrow morning, early nights all round'. Paul continued with his work as Tom went through to the kitchen to get a glass of water.

Frey was at the dining table with George's mother, Tania, and both were engaged in making decorations for the Elm tree in the close. 'Hello darling,' Frey said, as Tom walked in, 'what sort of a day have you had?' Frey stood up and walked over to him, and gave him a big hug and a kiss on the cheek. He could smell cooking on her. 'How's my little man?' Tom was a little embarrassed, especially seeing as Tania was there as well, and he could feel his face tingling red. 'Not bad…just been out to the woods with George and the others, what's for dinner? Oh Sorry, hello Tania, how are you?'

Tom felt a little guilty that he had forgotten himself. 'I'm very well thank you Tom, I understand you've been doing well at school, your Mother and Father have been telling me all about it'.

Tom didn't really know what to say, he could feel the tingling red sensation creeping up his cheeks and over his brow, and after an awkward exchange, and a quick glug of water, Tom shot off upstairs and got his robes out of the trunk at the end of his bed.

As he hung them up on the side of the wardrobe, he thought to himself, just another year, and I'll be recognised as a man. The *'Ritual of the Sun'*, which was held annually, was a two day event in which boys and girls who had turned 18 over the past year were initiated into the rights of adulthood. It wasn't that Tom disliked being a boy, there were many freedoms that came with being young, but he longed to be like his Father, strong, capable, and reassured. But he also felt a little guilty. In wanting to be a man he came over feeling as if he was rejecting his Mother's affection, and that the way she looked at him might change too. Once again, his parents' words of advice came to mind. 'Change is just a natural part of the balance of life, and balance is good, because everything in nature is balance.' Whenever Tom thought about this, he was always reminded of his Philosophy teacher, Miss Hope. She gave a lesson the previous year which had left most in the class, including Tom, a little bewildered. She had explained that "...out in the vastness of space there is something called a Black Hole. This Black Hole can take physical matter and stretch the very atoms it's made of beyond the remit of reality, and if you were to stand on the very edge of this Black Hole, the event horizon, you would be able to see the past, present, and future simultaneously in a single moment. Meanwhile, out in the rest of the universe, planets come and go, stars implode, and stars are born. Even the solar Gods of other galaxies eventually burn out after consuming the worlds around them. This, class, is the blueprint of the universe. This is its grand design, and for everything it destroys it creates something new, and vice versa. Down here on earth, we worry about such silly little things. Where am I going? What's for dinner? Does that boy like me? When really, all of existence is in flux, and subject to the same change as the rest of the universe. It is neither good or bad, because it is just the universe balancing itself out in accordance with its own directions.

The spark that initiated all of reality is the origin of all things, and carried all of the potential for things to come. That includes you, me, and everything. This means that you are simultaneously everything, because you share that common link, and nothing because you are so small in relation to the 'grand design'."

Ω

After everyone had had dinner, and finished prepping for the following day's events, it was these thoughts of manhood, change, the universe and the future, that sent the young boy off into a deep gentle sleep, with dreams of profound sunrises and jewel incrusted skies full of life, and all the wonders to behold.

Festival of Lights.

"Numerous shrines, sacred to a large number of gods, had been built on these outer rings"
(**Plato** – Timaeus and Critias)

Tom was awoken in the early hours of the morning by his Father, who gently shook his arm. Tom felt a burst of excitement at the sight of his Father, who was dressed in his dark brown robes, with brown sandals, and a belt around his waist with a small knife attached. His face was painted dark green, which made his eyes stand out like bright brown buttons on a smart jacket. 'Come on sleepy bones, time to get ready', he whispered.

Tom pulled the bed sheets back, and rubbed the sleep from his eyes. Having had a wash the night before, Tom excitedly put on his own robes and sandals, and applied a thick layer of green vegetable paint to his face. He gave himself the pleasure of a cursorily look in the mirror to check he had applied the paint evenly, then took a quick look out the window. The sun hadn't yet risen, and a blanket of stars still twinkled in the heavens. Excitement bubbled inside him, and the melancholy of the previous night had all but gone. Soon, all in the neighbourhood would be making their way up the hill of Minerva, towards the megalith.

$$\Omega$$

Tom thundered his way down the stairs and into the hall way, where Frey and Paul were waiting for him. His Mother was dressed in a long flowing white gown, with a crown of flowers placed gently on her plated golden hair. They both stood before him, hand in hand, and gently smiled at him. Tom stood at the foot of the stairs for a moment looking at his parents. In their eyes he could see nothing but love, warmth, and kindness. Even in the semi lite hall he could see his Mothers eyes glaze with tears. She stepped forward, knelt before her son, and looked up at him, taking him by the hand, 'My beautiful boy, I'm so proud of you.' The pair embraced, and Tom could feel a glowing brilliance dance inside his heart. His Father wiped a tear from his eye and cleared his throat of emotion. 'Come on then, lets join the others.'

$$\Omega$$

Outside the air was cool and crisp, and you would have mistaken it for still being night if the first tweets of the morning chorus couldn't already be heard in the distance. The whole of Yggdrasil close had formed outside in a long procession, women and girls at the front bearing lanterns, and the men and boys bringing up the rear, some with small drums under their arms.

Tom and his Father gave Frey a kiss before she went and joined the ranks of other lantern bearing women at the front of the procession, while Tom's Father escorted him into the ranks of the other men and boys.

When the last few had finely joined the procession, a beat was sounded on one of the drums, and the women began to chant. The eerie, hypnotic sound resonated around them, and in that moment nothing else existed. Time and space had stopped. Suddenly the procession began to move, and the drum beat increased, setting the pace. The women also began to chant louder, and soon the chants became song, long, drawn out lyrics that couldn't be discerned. Only women were allowed to learn the sacred words of the songs they sang, and understand the sacred feminine messages that they held.

Ω

Boom, boom, boom, the drums sounded louder again. Tom looked around to see if he could see his father, but he had disappeared into the thronging mass of brown robes and green faces. The only person he could make out was one of his neighbours, and that was only because he had such a prominent grey beard.

Again, the drum beats sounded, and ahead Tom could see the swaying lanterns, all lit in a variety of different colours, lovingly held by the women who continued to sing and chant.

Eventually the procession was moving through the countryside, and began to make its way up the hill towards the Megalith, the sun at last making itself present beyond the hill, silhouetting the great standing stone ahead of them. All around in various directions the lanterns from other groups of people could be seen in the distance, making their way across the landscape. And across the nation all citizens were joined in one motivated movement. A unified national consciousness of one mind, and one purpose.

In the early morning light, which was only very gentle, Tom could see the green of the grass beneath his feet lighten, and the glistening dew drops on each blade beginning to sparkle. It was a glorious sensation to feel the damp grass brush against his sandaled feet, and to smell the fresh earthy scent of a new morning.

When at last they had all reached the apex of the hill, the women moved in a single column, holding hands, and surrounded the great megalith at their centre.

The great stone structure loomed up out of the earth, and dominated the entire spectacle. Close to its base on each of its four sides were small alcoves, and placed in each alcove was a small figure, each one in a different colour. Red, blue, green and yellow.

As the women and girls swayed from side to side, still singing, the men and boys entered the centre of the circle and rotated around the megalith, each taking their time, and making sure that every one of the assembled males touched all of the figures in their little niches. Finally, when this had been completed, the men began to circulate among themselves, taking each other by the shoulder, and placing their hand on the others chest as a formal greeting and sign of brotherhood. Tom did as the others did, and when he came face to face with his father, a deeper, more profound message was felt between the two, a feeling and understanding that can only ever be felt between a loving son, and a devoted father.

As this ritual unfolded beneath the towering gaze of the great stone megalith, the sun had half risen on the horizon, sending out its glorious golden rays. The peak of the megalith which was caped in quartz, focused the rays of the sun and sent out beams of brilliant light out over the hill, like a beacon sending a message as if from heaven itself, to all who could see it.

Ω

When the men had eventually finished their ritual, the women dropped their hands to their sides and allowed the men to exit from the circle. As each man passed between the shoulders of two women, they uttered the words 'I am born', to which the women would reply, 'unto the earth'.

It was an incredible ritual to witness, one which was performed every summer, and had been for the last 400 years.

It wasn't just here, at the foot of the megalith that the people of Arcadia congregated on this special day. Other sacred spots, dotted around the countryside that surrounded Arcadia were numerous, and catered to a variety of different communities and the worship of different deities. In the glowing excellence of the rising sun, with a view to match, Tom could see the worshiper's lanterns at Thor's Lake on the far side of Arcadia in the distance, and to his left and right in some of the outlying woodland, the last twinkle of lantern light amongst the trees. Arcadia stood out of the landscape, a brilliant metropolis built in harmony with its surroundings, the tips of its buildings capped in the orange-red glow of a new day.

The Celebration.

"He that gives should never remember, he that receives should never forget"
(The Talmud)

Back at the close, all of Yggdrasil's residence were sitting at a huge table laid out in the middle of the road. The men, women, and children all sat where they pleased, with young and old all mixed together. Tom sat next to George, and the two yakked away about the morning's activities, while everyone else was busy discussing such varied topics as farming and politics, to Cherries and Apples. Dishes of food of varying sizes were also being handed around, and jugs of sweet amber mead and golden beer were constantly being refilled from giant barrels at the end of the table. The whole place was a buzz of laughter, happiness, and merry making.

Ω

The sun was high, and the sky was the sort of blue that only existed in paintings or pictures it was so beautiful. Tom looked up, and above him flew a magpie, quickly followed by a pair of gulls who, not being too fond of them, were evidently seeing it off in squawking fashion.

On the other side of the road, next to George's house, a Fox was creeping out from behind a large bush in the front garden, followed tightly by a pair of cubs. Evidently disturbed by the commotion, they probably thought it best to slink off while no one was looking. Even a few butterflies made an appearance at the table. Two small cabbage whites spun around each other in a gentle silent dance, while an even smaller blue one sat quietly on a freshly cut carnation that Mrs Summers had placed in a fluted white vase on the table. Tom couldn't find the words. It was just perfect.

Ω

'Can I have everyone's attention please? I say, could you all pipe down a tad I'd just like to say a few words?' From the end of the table, still dressed in his ceremonial garb, Mr Trent, who was on the Neighbourhood Commission, and one of very few men to be both employed in Council duties as well as being a priest, stood up and gesticulated with his plump reddening hands for everyone to be quiet.

After a few moments, quite ensued. 'Thank you' Mr Trent said with a small degree of relief. 'As you are all well aware, today marks not only the Festival of Light, but also the 150th anniversary of the building of Yggdrasil close. Now I know that this might only be a small community, but it's safe to say that this is a happy one. Now before you all start clapping and cheering and drinking more this very fine mead, I would like to say that as your local priest it is highly unorthodox for you to also vote for me to be your local representative on the Neighbourhood Commission. As we all know, Religion and Politics seldom make good bed fellows, but it fills me with such honour and joy that you might overlook such a thing, and trust me to perform my duties on behalf of you all. With this aside though, I would like to thank everyone for making this morning's ceremony so moving, and to all those who have contributed to the wonderful party we have here on this beautiful afternoon. So, I would like you to raise a glass…'. Everyone stood and raised a glass in the air, and repeated the toast as Mr Trent gave it. 'To Kin, to Soil, to our Forebears, and to the Panopticon'.

After a brief moment of standing reflection, everyone sat down and resumed their conversations and lunch.

Tom also continued his yakking with George, little knowing that tomorrow would raise questions, that would ultimately bring to light the true reality of the world he lived in.

Ω

Meanwhile, across the length and breadth of Arcadia, the sun pulled itself across the sky sending its warmth out to all that stood beneath it. The central districts of Arcadia were like a ghost town, with everyone either celebrating the Festival of lights with their respective communities, or out in the countryside enjoying the afternoon sun. On days like this, Arcadia's centre was given over to the wildlife, which roamed the empty streets. Deer, Birds, Rodents, all came out of the public gardens and made use of the vast and beautiful expanse of civilization.

A Walk in the Woods.

"The works of Fortune are not independent of Nature"
(**Marcus Aurelius** – *Meditations*)

The following morning, Tom was peering out of the living room window, watching as the last few remnants of the party were being swept up. It had been a wonderful day he thought to himself as he went into the kitchen to help his Mother with the breakfast. His Father was sitting at the table reading the paper and his Mother was busying herself by the cooker. The fresh smell of toast permeated the air, and the rays of morning light and bird song filled the kitchen with life. The signs of a new day.

Ω

'Can I help with anything', Tom asked. His mother turned her head over her shoulder towards him, 'no, everything is under control. Sit down and I'll bring your breakfast over.' Tom pulled up a chair and sat himself down at the table with his Father. After a second or two, Paul peered over the top of his paper, 'So, what's on the agenda today my boy?'
Paul always took a keen interest in whatever his son was up to. 'I'm not sure' Tom replied, 'I'm thinking of going for a walk in the woods, or maybe a trip to the library. I haven't made my mind up yet'.

Paul folded the paper in two and casually slung it onto the worktop next to him. 'You not spending the day with George?' Paul asked with an air of surprise. Tom looked down at the table as if considering the proposition. 'Well, after all the excitement yesterday I feel like being on my own today'. That was when Tom finalised his plan for the day, he would go for a walk in the woods. 'Well whatever your up to…' Toms Mother said, 'have your breakfast first'. She placed the bacon and toast down on the table in front of him, and as she walked away, she ran her hand lovingly over his hair.

Ω

An hour or so later Tom was strolling through beautiful oak woodland. He'd set off with the mind to see if he could get a closer look at the new squirrel population which his Teacher had told him were now thriving in the area. As he walked, his curiosity was rewarded.

About two meters away, curled around a tree, he noticed two red squirrels darting up and down the trunk, evidently chasing each other, with their beautiful rust coloured bodies twisting with the curve of the tree as they did so.

Tom watched them, and remembered what his Teacher had told him about their reintroduction about ninety years ago. It was lovely to start seeing them more regularly as the population increased. The grey variety had pretty much become extinct in Pretania, and only a few clusters of them remained. It was due, in part, to the Culling Initiatives introduced by the Panopticon, that saw large quantities of Non-Indigenous Invasive Species being effectively eradicated. Tom wasn't really sure how he felt about this, but he knew that the red squirrels had been near extinction in the British Isles for quite some time, and it was always a delight to see them.

His Teacher had explained that the Culling Initiatives had been a necessary evil, and after a few more probing questions from Tom he had to concede that 'the Initiative had been adopted for a number of other species, but at the end of the day it was all in the name of balance and harmony with the natural world.'

Whilst considering this, Tom turned his gaze to the ground, and among the leaves at the base of the tree he noticed the broken husks of acorns, and not too far from them a small cluster of delicate little blue flowers, with what looked to be something shinney between their leaves. What was it?

Ω

Wandering over, and bending down to get a closer look, he noticed that whatever it was between the delicate little leaves certainly wasn't anything natural. Picking at it carefully at first, checking it wasn't anything dangerous, he grasped it and gave it a good sharp tug. As the shinney, glistening sheet pulled away from the earth it took up half the plant with it, exposing its roots, and damaging one of the flower heads. Tom, unsure of what he held in his hands, just stared at it. It was some sort of small bag with heavily faded writing on it. It read 'Crunch'. What did it mean? Shoving the bag into his pocket, he knelt down and replanted what was left of the now pathetic little flower, stood up, and pressed his foot down against the earth to compact it around the roots. It still looked sad, but Tom was more interested in the shinney packet that he had in his pocket.

Ω

Tom ran with great excitement over to the edge of the wood, hoping that the sunlight would give him a better look at what was on the bag. He was so excited, that as he ran, he didn't even notice the other small clusters of flowers that he was treading on, pressing their fine features into the earth in a distorted mess beneath his feet. Nor did he notice the other pair of red squirrels that sat on a branch watching him rush past. It was all about the bag!

Ω

When he finally reached the edge of the woods, out of breath but full of curiosity, he pulled the bag from his pocket. He held it in both hands and moved it around in the light until it caught it just right that he could see the writing. '*Crunch Crisps. The crunchiest crisps around*!' Tom had no idea what it meant, and even less comprehension of what the bag was made of. Something halfway between paper and metal, but it hadn't been effected by the damp of the ground, so it couldn't be paper. Neither could it be metal, as it wasn't cold to the touch. It was unlike anything he had ever seen before in his life.

Toms first instinct was to take it home immediately and show his Father, he would know what it was. Tom thought of how pleased his Father would be that his son had discovered something so amazing! He carefully folded the packet in two and placed it back in his jacket pocket, and pated it gently to insure it was safe.

Ω

Rushing back through the woods in the direction of home, Tom thought of all the wonderful things his Mother and Father might tell him about the packet, and how clever he was to have found it. But the poor young boy couldn't have been further from the truth. Filled with an ecstasy of joy, Tom cleared the woods in minutes and was now bounding over the grasslands towards Yggdrasil close. His heart thumped in his chest and his lungs burned, but despite this he kept running and bounding over the land towards home, all the while thinking of the possibilities his discovery could make. He might even be able to show his teachers as part of a class project, or maybe the local paper would do an article on him.

Perhaps it would open up new avenues for him in some way. All these thoughts, and all these opportunities, none of which had ever crossed the young boys mind before. These, were alien thoughts…

Ω

When Tom had finally reached home, he flung the front door open, not even bothering to shut it behind him, much to the dismay of his mother who was just coming down stairs with a bundle of clothes to be washed. 'Erm, excuse me young man, have you forgotten something!?' She didn't look best pleased, Tom could tell.

Her tone was curt and quick. 'I'm sorry Mum, but where is Dad? I must show him something!'. Without even bothering to close the door, despite his Mother's protest, he ran into the kitchen and found Paul standing over the sink washing his hands.

Ω

Out of breath, and barely able to get his words out, he reached into his pocket and presented the shiny little packet to his father, beaming. 'Look what I found…isn't it incredible?' Paul looked down at what his son held in his hand. It only took a few seconds, but as Paul took the packet from Tom, and eyed it's crinkled metallic surface, his face turned from positive inquiry, to pale shame and sadness. He looked up from the packet, and addressed his son directly in the eyes, 'Where did you find this, Tom?'

Ω

Between Tom showing his Father the packet, and his Mother coming into the kitchen to ask what all the fuss was about, Paul had sat his Son down at the dining table, and asked Frey if she would join them. 'You say you found this in the woods, Tom?' Paul asked with probing precision.
 'Yes' replied Tom, 'and I thought you would…' but Tom was cut short by his Fathers retort. 'Right! Frey, I want you to call Mr. Wells at the Panopticon. Get him to notify the Woodland Preservation Department, and tell them we've found a Class 3-P Prohibited Item.

Whilst Frey ran down to the end of the close to use the public phone, Paul sat in silence looking down at the packet he'd placed on the table between them. 'Ok Tom, now I know this all seems a bit of a panic, but do you know what you've found, and why we are so concerned?' Tom hung his head in shame, 'No, I don't'. His tone indicated he was on the verge of tears, and he could feel a rumbling swell building in his throat and chest. He had no idea what was going on, but he knew it was serious.

The last time he'd seen his Father this way was three years ago, when there had been some altercation with a previous neighbour over something to do with the Communal Recycling. The authoritative tone was the same. The sharp needle like enquiry, punctuated with long staring evaluation.

After a moment or two Paul calmed down, and placed his hand on Tom's knee in a reassuring, and understanding manner. 'Ok, I know this isn't your fault, and you didn't know what you were doing, but I must stress the magnitude of what has happened here.

Now, you're a smart young man, and I know you will listen to what I have to say before you start asking questions.' Tom nodded acquiescence. And thus, began the Lesson. 'Where to begin?

A History Lesson.

"Especially unique to man is the search and scrutiny into truth"
*(**Cicero** – On Obligations)*

'What we have here Tom, is a plastic bag. To be more precise, it looks like a bag that might have contained some sort of food related product, but we'll find out more when it's analysed by the Panopticon. This sort of thing was very common in the days of our ancestors that predated the Tipping Wars. I'm sure your teachers have told you all about it, and how evil this substance is? This stuff is barely used anymore, and if it is, in the smallest of quantities, and only for very specific reasons, like research, or for essential components in technology.

Even then, we have alternatives that are infinitely more bio-network friendly. If you can imagine this Tom, that nearly whole portions of the ocean were swimming in this stuff! Animals, and Humans alike were plagued with literal mountains of plastic rubbish. And why? Because at the end of the day, our ancestors were lazy. Not ignorant, just plain lazy and selfish. From what we understand, they were only interested in quick fix ideas, and satisfying they're immediate needs without a care for the repercussions.

And plastic was only the beginning. Pollution on a scale that you could only imagine. So bad, that some people in parts of the world were literally chocking to death on the toxins that were supposed to make their lives easier! Something often referred to as Rock Fuel.

Plastic wasn't the only thing, but what it represents to us, today, is a past that we don't want to return to. A past that could have destroyed our future… I understand that these things won't have been talked about in any depth at school, not until you're a little older, but given the circumstances I think it's important for you to know the score.

Now, my Grandfather, Tom. He was a good man, and a shinning example to us all. Anything the community needed, he did. If a fellow citizen needed a hand with something or was in some sort of difficulty, he was there. What I suppose you would call a real pillar of the community. One day, he noticed that one of his neighbours had left a small pile of rubbish in his back garden. It was nothing of any magnitude, just some worn out kitchen utensils and some old wood beams from the attic. He politely said to this neighbour that all of these items were recyclable goods, and why not pop them in the communal bins so they could be taken away to be repurposed.

Needless to say, he took no notice and continued to pile up all sorts of rubbish in his garden. One day, my Grandfather knocked on his door, and said that if any other neighbours were to see what he'd been doing, then they would surely notify the authorities, and he would probably get into some sort of trouble! Do you know what his neighbour said? "Mind your own business!", and slammed the door in his face. Now, my grandfather was a very patient man, and made several appeals to him to sort through the rubbish and recycle it. He knew that if the Panopticon was to find out, he could at the very least incur a heavy fine, or at worse, public shame and disgrace. My Grandfather wanted to save him from that.

Ω

Needless to say, the Panopticon did find out. And he did indeed incur a big fine. But did he change his ways? No, he didn't. In fact it made things worse, and rather than just creating large rubbish piles in his garden, he started burning what he could on large bonfires. You may wonder what all the fuss was about, but when you think that all of that rubbish could have been used for other proposes to befit the rest of society, like running a generator that helps pump water to the communal wells, you can begin to see the problem.

Several more fines, and two hearings later, it was decided that he would face the ultimate punishment. Seeing as Prisons had been abolished about two hundred years previous, because it was obvious that they weren't working in the rehabilitation of criminals, he was made an example of. His two sons were refused admittance to the academy, and three subsequent generations after them. He on the other hand, met no punishment other than the shame and misery of knowing that his actions had immediately affected not only his own sons, but future generations that he would never know. As you can imagine, his family barely spoke to him again.

What is the moral of the story here? Just as our ancestors acted without a care for the future and left us with the monumental task of undoing all the harm they had caused, so too would his sons have to work in jobs bellow their station, despite being eligible for the academies, to undo the sins of their father.

Ω

I guess what I'm trying to say Tom, is that the past has a very definite impact on the future, and the repercussions can be felt for generations. For example, The Tipping Wars, they should never have happened, but they did, and it was necessary. A battle of wills between the selfish and the righteous. A battle of ideas, that could have gone in either direction. This is why the *Pretanic Isles* are the way they are today. Great men and women, making great decisions, for the greater good! That's how the Panopticon was born, as I'm sure you know, when the very best of the people at the highest levels of their field were brought together to make the decisions for the rest of us. Don't get me wrong, democracy is a fine thing, but when you think about what it allows people to do with their lives, you begin to see how some people can't be trusted with such freedoms. You need people in control who know what they are doing. This is why we have what is called an 'Eco-Senateocracy'. I won't lie to you, as you get older and progress through your academic career, you'll learn more about this, and the dark history that this nation is responsible for, and how far we have had to go in order to restore a sense of peace, harmony, and order. A process which is still ongoing to this day. If you think about the Recovery Zones dotted across this nation, they act as a reminder that even now, nearly a thousand years later, these intense issues still resonate today. Those areas were so horribly devastated by humanities lack of care, that they are now off limits to but a few people who work on re-establishing some sense of natural balance in these zones, through hard work and graft. As for the rest of us, it's a no-go area, and we must endure the fact that we will never have the chance of visiting these places in our life time.

Ω

What you found today was a small reminder of this past. You never know, the Panopticon could easily decree that because of what you found in the woods, they are now going to review that area as a potential Recovery Zone, and as a consequence shut it off to fellow citizens until further notice if they find anything else.

Ω

It would be foolish of me to make you think that this was just a problem here in Pretania, but of course, it's not. The whole of Europa was awash with the same problems. Take Germania for example. Just prior to The Tipping Wars, it was a dreadful place!

It had built such a vast infrastructure of industry and commerce, and imported such enormous quantities of foreign goods, that it eventually fell apart under the weight of its own success. Everybody at that time wanted a slice of the pie, and people flocked from all over East and West Europa to get it. As a result of such large numbers of people, they had some of the largest principal land-fill sites in the world! I'm sure you have learnt about what these are? So many non-degradable products were being produced and discarded on a daily basis that they were forced to send ever increasing amounts of their own rubbish to other countries for disposal. As if this wasn't bad enough, many other European nations had tried to follow the Germainian economic blueprint, and so all the other nations in Europa were sending their own rubbish to far and distant lands, in the hope of being able to ignore the problem. Can you imagine it, Tom? The sheer stupidity of some people, that they think they are doing the right thing by sending rubbish elsewhere? It's still on the planet! It hasn't actually gone anywhere at all!

In fact, it's worth noting that the ecological short falls of our ancestors weren't the only issue. In the times leading up to The Tipping Wars, there were mass cultural and societal breakdowns.

Everything had become cheap and degraded. Nothing of any cultural or spiritual value was held in any real regard. People just stopped caring about anything that wasn't physically pleasurable, or monetary. We're not really too sure what caused this, but it appears that there had been a number of international catastrophes that had lead people, over the course of a few centuries, to abandon many on the binding traditions that helped them relate to the earth, and each other as fellow human beings. In the West, one of these traditions is something they called *Testament,* or *The Gospel*. Unfortunately, little of these traditions survive today for us to be able to understand them. This is what eventually culminated in The Tipping Wars, and The Great Exodus. People were living miserable and soulless lives that hinged on such pathetic and uninspiring foundations. They had concocted a whole host of strange pursuits, just to relieve themselves of the horror of their own existence, but at the same time making it worse! To give you an example of how morally and spiritually bankrupt these people were, evidence has been found in old documents from the era, and archaeological finds, that suggests these people had so much freedom, that they were altering their physical appearance with plastic

inserted under their skin. They were physically putting plastic into themselves! How desperate and miserable must these people have been? Just think of how these people must have perceived themselves and the people around them? They must have been both shallow, and very sad to behold. If this wasn't bad enough, they prolonged the agony of the elderly too, by insisting on them living beyond their years. Millions of elderly people were made to suffer. Not like today, where we ensure the very best support for our elderly through the 'Fellowship'. When individuals reach a certain age, we allow them to die naturally, and make sure they get the best of care up to that point. Not left to live on and on in pain and agony, while the rest of society enjoys the benefits of youth.
We understand, that natures balance can't be tampered with. All things must return to the source… Our ancestors saw death as a taboo.

Ω

Eventually, people became detached, and fragmented. So much so, that they fell into decay and depression. The artificial nature of their own lives and the world they inhabited nearly spelt their destruction. Something had to give…

It's safe to say that as a result of this, they eventually began to band together again for mutual reassurance and support, and questions began to be asked of the governments and corporations that had allowed this all to happen. Of course, it wasn't long before people began to realise that the blame wasn't completely on the shoulders of those in charge, and ultimately it was 'The People' who were the ones who had allowed themselves to become corrupted by the powers that be, and given themselves over to greed and selfishness.

$$\Omega$$

At first it was only a few radical groups who began leaving Europa for distant shores, with the intent of leading simpler lives, in tune with the ebb and flow of nature. Many people of Africainian decent, so it is said, left for the continent we now call Eden, where they deposed corrupt governments and installed a system which sort to value the lives of animals and plants more important than that of humans. Admirable, I must say. Even today, it is illegal to enter the continent of Eden without express international approval, for fear that its beautiful balance be disrupted.

It has been said, by some of our greatest scholars, that many of the Africainian people had been so horribly treated by the people of Europa, that they decided to leave once and for all, and let the Europeans deal with the mess that they had created for themselves. Though how true this is, we're not completely sure.

Ω

Despite this, after the first initial Exodus many people started getting ideas about what they could do to help improve matters. Many more acts of Exodus began to happen, and many people just upped sticks and moved away. Where people found a community that suited them, that's where they stayed. Soon people began working together again and formulating plans on how to undo all the dreadful things that had happened.

I'm not too sure how it really happened, because the history books are a little vague on this point, but it seems that new and old traditions that people thought to be of good value were brought together depending on the region they had settled in.

For example, a number of Europeans moved in the direction of a place that was referred to as Zion, and even though they had no connection to this place, they converted to the traditions of that land and helped in the building of an important temple that was sacred in the traditions of those people. Others though, stayed put and did what they could where they were situated.

Ω

Pretania is pretty much one of those places where most people stayed put and did what they could. Sure, there were a few Exoduses in the early days, but on the whole people stuck to the earth they knew and loved. That's probably why its worked. Our more recent descendants harkened back to a time when the people were bound to the earth in such an intrinsic way, that they saw themselves as a part of the soil itself. They re-invigorated the traditions of *Mos Maiorum*, and found themselves bound to a duty of preservation and unity. Your hero, Tom. Dr Galahad Foresight Perkins, was the man who gave us the great rally call and inspirational speech we call *Design for Life*.

He, and others like him, brought about some of the first great initiatives that got the ball rolling, and started to make us think more about the world we inhabited. *'Design for Life'* is what we did. We built on the principle of living, not existing.

So many of the towns and cities were rebuilt or adapted along lines that made cohesion between Human, Stone, Plant, and Animal more harmonious, and the ancient texts that survived the great upheavals of the past, by authors such as Plato, Orwell and Dickens, were made compulsory reading for children, in the hope that it would instil in them a sense of moral and ethical fortitude, whilst at the same time help them understand the true meaning of benevolence.

Ω

So, when we look at something as simple as plastic, we can start to see how something, however small it is, if abused, can be part of the genesis of something terrible.'

Ω

When Tom's Father had finally finished, Frey, who had been listening in the living room ever since she got back from the phone call, came into the kitchen and stood behind Paul, her hands on his shoulders. They both looked at Tom with a look that understood that he had been made privy to more than young boys of his age should be. Part pity, and part understanding was how they looked at him, and they noticed that in the intervening time between Tom's childish sprints across the meadow, to who he was now, sitting at the kitchen table, a piece of Tom was no more. Something had flown before its time, never to return.

Et in Arcadia Ego.

"alea iacta est"
(Julius Caesar)

Embarrassment and shame. Pure and simple. Tom had never truly felt this before, not like this! He had always been 'master of the A grade', and 'oracle of the answers', but this time he'd got it wrong, very wrong indeed. That sense of pride that he'd worn like a flowing purple cloak had been torn from his naked shoulders, and exposed him for the fragile boy that he was. It hurt.

Not only had his foolish pride got in the way of him thinking straight, but it had been exposed by the very people who he thought he could always turn to for reassuring words. The fact that his father had told him some of the worse things he could possibly imagine as the result of him finding something in complete ignorance, made next to no sense at all.

Tom decided to blow the cobwebs away with a trip into town, and rather than catching the tram, he decided to take a leisurely walk instead, and hoped that a nice long stroll and a visit to the Museum might help relieve the tension that was beginning to swell in his chest.

The 'Via Cincinnatus' was the main road into, and out of Arcadia from Yggdrasil Close, and was the only means, other than walking cross country, of getting from one point to the next. It was flanked by Plane trees, which hung their branches over the road and offered those on foot natural cover from the sun in high summer. Beyond the trees, for the most part, was a wide expanse of grassland periodically broken up with woodland, some of which was dedicated to wildlife preservation and re-wilding, and depending on the time of year, could be off limits if rare species of plants, or animals had been found in the area. If Tom had been looking where he was going, he would have noticed a deer ambling calmly across the road and into the field on the other side, but he was too busy looking down at the pavement, with his thoughts locked into an eternal loop of why's and how's.

When eventually Tom reached the outskirts of Arcadia, he had been walking for just over half an hour, most of which had been spent with his hands dug deep into his pockets, and his head slung low. The eternal loop had not subsided, but what drew Tom's attention away from the desperation of his predicament was the sounds and smells of the Workshop district on the periphery of town.

The road changed from gravel composite to cobbles, which had been recycled from the 'old times', and passing through the district, Tom could hear the clanging of hammer against metal, and the rough drone of saws cutting through wood, which gave off a rich dusty smell and it was cut. To Tom, the smell often carried with it the promise of something new, but in his present state his usually upbeat philosophical view of things had become muted and dull. The workshops were trapezoidal, single story, and tightly grouped, helping them conform to the cylindrical nature of Arcadia, and played host to a number of different artisanal trades. As he passed one of the workshops he quickly glanced inside. Two men stood over an anvil, one with a large ballpein hammer, and the other holding a pair of large pliers in gloved hands. Tom had just enough time to see that their faces were black with coke, and their thick leather aprons heavy with dirt hanging stiffly around their necks.

A few yards away a stone mason was working under cover of a small porch, evidently benefiting from the natural light, and was gently tapping away at a section of granite with a lettering chisel. As Tom passed, the mason looked up and smiled, but Tom was in no mood. He just nodded assent, and moved on towards the centre of Arcadia.

The sun poured itself down on the town, and gave Arcadia's commercial district, which Tom was now entering, an almost ethereal glow. The angular, robust features of the shop fronts ennobled the products inside for sale, and the whole of that part of town was awash with all sorts of people, buying, selling, and some simply enjoying the hustle and bustle of commerce. It was one huge organic mass of people, moving and operating in a chaotic form of harmony. One of the shops, on Tom's right and next to a tram stop was selling fruit and vegetables, all seasonal and locally grown, from underneath a striped canvas awning. Next to that was a shop that dealt primarily in children's clothes, from ages 5 to 18, and as per Panopticon decree, provided *'clothes applicable to function, and in keeping with the sanctity of innocence'*. There was no discussion on this decree, it was just understood. Opposite, on the other side of the road, stood a large double fronted building with Ionic styled columns over hung by a dominant and ornate pediment. It was one of about 30 book shops in Arcadia, selling primarily academic works, but also children's books and repair manuals, obviously in the interests of promoting a form of self-sufficiency that was encouraged in these times. Some of the books were age restricted, such as history books, and an I.D was needed for their purchase.

All the shops, as far as Tom could see, were thronging with people, and the pavements were packed. Tom felt dizzy. The hustle and bustle of the commercial district, which was normally a treat, had an oppressive vibe about it, and the sun just seemed to intensify the oppressive feelings brewing in Tom's mind. He quickly checked no trams were coming in either direction, and made a break for it across the road, and down one on the side streets towards the centre of Arcadia.

One of the interesting features of Arcadia, was that like so many towns of its type it had very strict opening times for its shops. It didn't matter if it was a fresh produce merchant or a tool shop, all stores were shut on Saturn-Day and Sun-Day, and during the week shops were open early, from between 5:30/6:00am, and shut promptly at 3:30pm. The reason for this was that people were encouraged to spend as much time as possible with their friends and family, or pursuing more enriching activities other than just window shopping or spending money. This wasn't law, it was just advice from the Panopticon, and people could do as they pleased, but the sense of social responsibility was so over powering, that they would no more stay open for an addition hour than throw their rubbish onto the pavement.

Finally, out of the way, and leaving the heaving masses behind him, he made his way down 'The Way of Hero's', and into the Academic district. Passing the statue of Dr G.F. Perkins without even a glance, he made a beeline for the Museum of Culture. By this point Tom didn't really know what he was doing. He felt compelled by some unknown force to get away from everything, and at the same time find sanctuary in something familiar. The Museum of Culture was bound to be empty at this time of day, and would have the peace and quiet Tom was looking for. It would also be cool and refreshing inside, and take the edge off the intensity of the sun.

Tom stopped just shy of the stereobate leading up and into the Museum. Turning, and allowing his eyes to gently role across the Academic district, it was quiet and calm. The whole area was wide and open, and at its heart, standing higher than any of the other buildings, was the Panopticon. Unlike any of the other buildings in Arcadia, the Panopticon was built along the Corinthian style of architecture, giving it a far grander, far more ornate appearance with its deep undulating floral designs on its capitals. Tom just stood in awe for a few minutes, hoping that the scene would calm his anxiety. To a certain extent, it did.

There was something reassuring about it, something grounded, something firm and reliable. Every major town had its own Panopticon and board of specialists and magistrates. The main Panopticon was located in the capitol, Londinium, and although it had no jurisdiction over the provinces, still past occasional decrees on social and cultural observances.

His thoughts were broken by some movement behind him. As he turned, he noticed two men walking down the steps from the Museum, both were dressed in their robes of office. One had a red sash that ran from his right shoulder down to his waist on his left, and in his right hand he carried a large book. Tom recognised him immediately as *Quaestor,* and one who was responsible for some of the financial and legal duties of Arcadia. The other man, who was a little older and probably in his mid-sixties, wore a green sash with purple trim, and carried in his right hand a bundle of scrolls, and a large wood bound codex.

Again, Tom knew immediately who this was, a high official at the Panopticon. Not a specialist, but probably a *Praetor* who had civil and provincial jurisdiction.

Ω

The two men noticed Tom, but didn't acknowledge him. It wouldn't have been proper to do so. Tom dropped his left hand to his side, placed his right hand over his chest, and took a long, deep bow. Tom held himself there for a couple of seconds, and when he righted himself, the younger of the two men raised his empty hand in greeting and nodded. Tom nodded too, and as they passed him and made their way slowly across the paved grounds towards the Panopticon, Tom gathered himself together, and made his way up the steps and into the cooling embrace of the Museum.

Ω

The internal structure of the Museum was much like that of Arcadia itself. Cylindrical in nature, each floor contained not only displays of relics from the past, but also book cases filled with numerous volumes for reading. Each floor had access to a central railed off section that looked down onto the ground floor where neatly organized rows of research desks were placed, so that visitors could take a book, or with special permission, an artifact, and spend time studying there. The smell of the Museum was part of its charm, and Tom always noted that it had a musty warmth about it. 'The smell of learning', his father would often say.

In the same way that book shops prohibited the sale of some books to children, it was the same in the library. The books that were off limits were kept in locked glass fronted wooden cabinets, and you needed a key from the receptionist at the Museum entrance if you wanted access. Tom, once again thinking about what his farther had said, and also feeling the swelling bulb of anxiety ballooning again his chest, felt an overwhelming desire to go up to the third floor where these cabinets were. Crossing to the other side of the Museum, past the research desks, he slowly made his way over to the cast iron spiral staircase that ran the entire four floors of the building. Knowing that he needed to keep as quiet as possible, so as not to disturb the other visitors, he walked up the stairs briskly, but on the balls of his feet, placing his feet as gentle as possible with each step up. Despite having been told that there was no need to go up to the third floor, as he would never have access to the books anyway, he knew he was going against convention. But a part of him didn't care. Much in the same way as he'd run through the woods, crushing flowers under foot as he went, he was overcome by a morbid drive to find out more about what his father had told him.

His right hand held the cold brass railing as he ascended, its freshly polished gleaming surface reflecting a distorted image of Tom as he went.

He finally reached the third floor. It was quiet. Only one other person was up there, an elderly man standing by one of the book cases and poring over a thick volumed book. Tom peered at him through the glass windowed wooden door, and carefully, trying not to make too much noise, gently pushed the door open and went inside.

Ω

Here he was, amongst the 'unmentionables'. He paused, making sure no one was looking, and gently moved over to the first case. A small sign stuck out from the top most corner of the cabinet. It read, *'Case 1, A-C. Abortion-Criminals'*. Tom only had a very mild understanding of what these words could have alluded to. He looked at the spines of the volumes behind the glass. He couldn't quite believe his eyes! The first one read *'Abortion in Review-(Infanticide in the early 20th century)'*. Tom could feel a hot embarrassment creeping up his cheeks at the thought it! Moving on to the end of the case, he read some of the other spines as he went:

Brothers without Faces- (The Death of the Family)

Bringers of Hate- (The Rape of the Natural World)

Criminal Justice in the Mid 21st Century Vol 1- (The Reintroduction of Hanging)

Cremation Vol 3- (The Destruction of the Amazon Rainforest)

The list went on. As Tom quietly made his way from one case to the next, the chapters got more and more horrific. Books on the mutilation of the human body, and volume after volume of different species of animals that had been made extinct.

He moved on to the next case. Again, much as before, it was filled with numerous volumes, some old, and some new. Each one had a more strange and perplexing title than the last. *'Dunes of the Sahara – (Eden's politics and Customs)'*. As he moved along the second case, he heard footsteps behind him, and the creaking of the wooden floorboards. It was coming from the direction of the elderly man he saw when he came in. Tom moved quietly over to the case behind him, doing his best not to make a sound and peered around the corner, trying not to be seen. The old man had gone. But that wasn't what interested Tom. What caught the young boy's attention was the open cabinet that had been left unattended!

Tom's eyes bulged with morbid intrigue, and despite the little voice at the back of his mind telling him to leave and go home, he stepped out from the shadow of the large bookcase he was standing behind, and crept over to where the old man had been standing, and the open cabinet door. He looked over his shoulders a couple of times, and then gingerly picked up the vast volume that had been left on a small table next to the case. It was heavy and dusty, and carried a smell somewhere between caramel, and ink. He turned the book over and read the spine, *'Four Seasons of the Sun- (An Exploration into the Pagan Rights of the Past)'*. Tom's intrigue was peaked, and he flicked through the vast volume, looking at all the various pictures and drawings it contained, periodically looking over his shoulder to check he wasn't being watched. After a few minutes, he put the book back down on the little table in the same position he had found it, and having placed a finger on the page that it was left open on when he picked it up, made sure that it was left open in the same place. If that was the sort of thing that could be found in this case, what else might there be?

Peering at the other dusty collections, a slim green volume jumped out at him. It wasn't like the others, it looked far older, and had gold printing down the spine that had faded and was unintelligible. Tom reached out, braced his index finger against the top edge of the book, and pulled it out. The print on the front cover was just as faded as on the spine, and he took it over to the light of a reading desk at the end of the case. **'The Sins of the Father– (Animal Cruelty and Profit)'.** The book was old, and judging from the poor condition of the binding had evidently been well thumbed.

Ω

A jarring twinge pulsed at the base of Tom's neck, and he felt a rising pressure build behind his eyes and in his temples. He pushed the sensation aside, rolled his shoulders, and cautiously opened the book.
The moment he saw the first disturbing picture, he wished he hadn't! It was a black and white photograph of a fox being stripped of its fur, wrenched and pulled at by two shabby looking men. The caption underneath said, *'Skinned alive. The practice of fur farming in Asia. C. 1983'.*

Tom brought his hand up to mouth, he thought he was going to be sick. A surging acidic sensation gurgled in his throat. He flipped the page over, trying to rid himself of the sight, but it just exposed more horrifying pictures.

This time, it was a picture of a small mouse being crushed under what looked like a large boot. Tom's eyes rolled down to the caption, '*A Brutal Act. A still from the film* **'Holocaust'**. *C. 2030'*. Tom felt a welling of tears building at the base of his eyes, and a sharp stinging sensation bouncing around his nostrils.

Tom didn't know why, but he kept flipping from one page to the next, and each time a new and more disturbing image presented itself. The final picture, the last straw, was of an enormous aquatic animal Tom didn't recognize. It was sprawled out on a huge dock, with its underbelly cut open and its skin baking dry in the midday sun. Again, the caption read '*Basking Shark, found off the coast of the Pretanic Isles. Thought to be the result of an Oil Tanker Spill. C. 1993'*

Ω

Tom couldn't quite understand. His mind filled with images that stained the backs of his eyes so that they remained there permanently, burnt into his thoughts. Cold, clammy sweat began to pearl on his forehead, and his chest tightened up like a compressed spring. He stood there, his mind looping over the perpetual thought of the baby mouse being crushed under a large boot…

Ω

As the images played back to him again and again, Tom sensed a presence behind him. It snapped him out of his thoughts, and he whirled around to see one of the white shirted Museum attendants looking down at him over her rimless glasses with a stern and authoritative look on her face. Before the attendant could say anything, Tom threw the book down and bolted for the door. It wasn't the thought of getting in trouble that propelled him into flight, but the want to get as far away from the museum as possible, and the dreadful new ideas that had entered his mind.

He scrambled down the tight spiral staircase, nearly tripping several times as he went. When he reached the bottom, the bounding of his feet drummed on the wooden floor boards of the museum, sending an echoing clatter across the entire building. Tearing past one of the research desks, he sent a huge pile of papers flying into the air and all over the floor.

He slammed himself into the doors that gave exit to the Museum, nearly knocking over a young female *Tribune* as he went, and leapt down the stairs and into the sun.

He didn't even bother to see if the young lady was ok, as he tore across the Academic district, and bolted for the safety of the Union Garden on the other side of the grounds. All the while he ran, the terrifying thoughts and pictures that his mind had been exposed to played out, over and over again, chasing his mind to the brink of insanity. Not only this, but the things his Father had said swirled around him, flashing images of mutated figures and toxic fumes being pumped into the air. Fish floating lifeless down sludgy streams, and the loneliness of individuals, forced to live lives of solitude against the pounding and fragmentary ideas of an out-of-control state!

Ω

When he did finally reach the Union Garden, out of breath, and desperate for relief, he threw himself down into the shade of one of the wooden tool sheds, brought his knees up to his chest, and pushed his horror-stricken face hard into the heavy canvas weave of his trousers, whilst rocking himself anxiously back and forth, to the jolting tune of his horror.

Something to Think About.

"Refrain from following the example of those whose craving is for attention, not their own improvement"
*(**Seneca** – Letters from a Stoic)*

A few days had passed since Tom's Father had given him the lecture, and his horrific visit to the Museum, and he had spent them in a bit of a daze. Toms Mother could see that he wasn't his normal self, but not wanting to interrupt an evidently forming moment in her sons understanding of the world, left him alone to his thoughts. She was unaware of his visit to the Museum of Culture, but she desperately wanted to hold him, and tell him that everything was ok, but she knew that despite this education coming a little earlier than it should have done, it was important to allow him some space. Tom's Father on the other hand had started to treat him less like a child, and more like a young man, something that for Tom had come as another shock. He had felt a distinct change in himself over the past year, that was for sure, but the sudden discovery of the plastic packet, the firm lecture on aspects of their collective history, the secret trip to the third floor of the Museum and the sudden change in the way his parents were treating him, made everything all the more intense. The questions were unending.

Ω

Something else was different too, but for the life of him he couldn't tell what it was. A weight had come to bear down on him, unrelenting, just sitting hard and firm on his shoulders.

Rather than mope around the house, he thought it best to spend his time in the company of George. At least that way he knew his mind would be taken of the issue.

'I'm just heading over to see George, Mum. I'll be back in a few hours.' He didn't even wait for a response. He already had his jacket in his hands and was out the door, and across the close.

Not five minutes later, Tom and George were strolling across the meadow that backed the close, deep in conversation. The sky was grey and overcast, and even though it wasn't cold, there was an uninviting breeze on the air. Tom had been telling George all about the last few days, and the whirlwind that had been unleashed ever since he'd found the plastic packet.

'So, you're saying your Father told you off for finding it?' George asked with his usual scruffy curiosity. 'Do you still have it? can I see it? what does it look like?' The questions came like a volley of gunfire, and very little time was given for explanation before another volley was unleashed.

Tom raised his hand in objection, irritated by the bombardment of questions. 'Wait wait wait!' Tom replied, with an air of aggression.

Tom began to regret having even mentioned the damn thing. 'I don't have it anymore, so no, you can't see it! And in all honesty, I don't even want to think about what it looks like. The whole thing has just been one big mess, and....' Tom paused, and stood on the spot looking down at his feet. His face dropped, and his shoulders sagged.

Ω

Staring down at his shoes against the rich brown earth and straw-coloured grass, an overwhelming desperation came over him, and nothing felt real. It was as if all reality as he knew it had been thrown into the air and scattered to the wind. For the first time in days tears began to roll uncontrollably down his face, and he slumped to the ground on his knees and began to cry. The pressure and weight of the past few days came rushing out of him with an intensity he had never known in his life, deep from within his soul.

George realised he had probably underestimated the severity of the situation. Not knowing what to do, and not knowing what to say, he did what any friend would do in the circumstances, he slumped down to the ground too, placed his arms around Tom's shoulders, and cried with him.

Their love for each other was so honest and pure that words would never have done. They just sat there together on the ground and wept, holding each other close, in a bond of comradeship and brotherly understanding.

Ω

After a few minutes, when Toms tears had finally ceased, and the agonising anxious pressure in his chest had subdued, he wiped his face on the cuff of his jacket. His eyes were red a sore from all the crying. He looked over to George, who more than anything wanted to say something, but for the first time in his life words failed him. Tom could see the confusion in his eyes. 'Don't worry George, I'm ok. I think I just needed to get it all out of my system.' Tom sat up a little and breathed a great sigh of relief. It was as if the tears had cleansed him, and washed away the last vestiges of something that was no longer him, like a butterfly casting off its cocoon.

As he wiped the last of his tears off on his sleeve the clouds parted, and the sun threw its wonderful golden fingers out onto the meadow, changing the dreary threads of grass into golden locks of splendor, wafting gently in the afternoon breeze. Tom closed his eyes, and basked in the brilliance of the sun's warmth. It was then, in the golden field, with his best friend's hand on his shoulder that he then realised.

The weight he'd felt over the past few days, and the changing face of his own existence. It was the burden of not just knowing, but the burden that he would now have to carry with him for the rest of his life. The burden of knowledge and responsibility. An adult burden. The idea hit Tom like a thunderbolt of realization, bursting into his mind with all the spectrums of colour he could imagine.

Ω

Tom looked at George with a regard that George had never seen before. 'What's up?' He asked, feeling as though Tom was about to do something unexpected.

Tom smiled, and his eyes were full and alive. Standing up, he pulled George up by the hand. 'George, sometimes knowing something can change you, and you're never sure if that change is good until you understand what that something is. I think I know now what my Father was trying to explain to me.' George looked at Tom in puzzlement. 'What do you mean?' George enquired.

'What I mean is, Our burden might not have been made by us personally, but it's ours to carry none the less. We are the ones who are responsible, not just for the past, but for where our future is headed. It's a heavy burden, but a good one because it's built on the principle and foundation of something worth carrying. And if we work together, we can all ease that weight which would cripple us if we had to bear it alone. We all have a responsibility to help carry it, not just for ourselves, but for others too. I know I'm not making it very clear, but do you see what I'm trying to say?'
George looked at Tom, even more puzzled than before. Tom smiled, and put his arm around George. 'Come on, I'll explain on the way home'.

If someone had been watching, they would have seen the two lads strolling happily off into the distance, while the warming embrace of the sun, which had finally broken through the clouds and settled on the golden threads of the meadow, carried with it all the promise of tomorrow.

$$\Omega$$

"You may leave this life at any moment: have this possibility in your mind in all that you do or say or think"
(**Marcus Aurelius** – *Meditations*)

A-The End**-Ω**

-Other Publications by This Author-

-About the Author-

Benjamin James Elliott was born in England in 1988, and currently resides in East Sussex. He is a philosopher, as well as an author of poetry and short stories, and having studied *Classics* at university, has incorporated much of these idealistic principles into his work.
He is a collector of antiquities and curios, and enjoys spending his time on the South Downs, which he tirelessly works to promote and protect.

Printed in Great Britain
by Amazon